W9-AAF-903

PUSS in BOOTS

Remember the wily cat in the bright yellow boots who used his head to make his master's fortune? Here's a chance to savor his exploits anew as Tony Ross recreates this popular story in a fresh, witty version.

The devilishly humorous full-color illustrations join with the droll text to bring to life innocent Jack, the lovely princess, the terrible ogre, and most of all Puss, the redoubtable ally whose schemes turn his master into a prince.

As with Tony Ross's recent *Jack and the Beanstalk* (also published by Delacorte Press), readers of all ages will rejoice at the rediscovery of an old favorite in bright new clothes.

PUSS in BOOTS

The Story of a Sneaky Cat

Adapted and Illustrated
by

Tony Ross

Delacorte Press/New York

For Mum and Dad

Published by
Dell Publishing Co., Inc.
1 Dag Hammarskjold Plaza
New York, New York 10017

This work was first published in Great Britain in 1981 by
Andersen Press Ltd.

Printed in Italy
First U.S.A. printing

Library of Congress Cataloging in Publication Data

Ross, Tony.
  Puss in boots.

  Summary: A clever cat wins his master a splendid
palace and the hand of a princess.
  [1. Fairy tales. 2. Folklore—France] I. Title.
PZ8.1.R693Pu 398.2'452974428'0944 [E] 81-2181
ISBN 0-440-07122-4   AACR2
ISBN 0-440-07157-7 (lib. bdg.)

Long, long ago, a miller lived in a mill with his three
sons. The eldest son was called Lazy Harry, the
second eldest was called Good-for-Nothing Tom, and the
youngest was called Jack. The miller also had a cat
with wild yellow eyes. His name was Puss.

Young Jack did all the work, but he did it happily, and
loved everyone and everything. He was sad when the
old miller fell sick.

When the miller died, he left the mill to Harry,
the horse to Tom, and the cat to Jack. Jack felt that
perhaps he was not so lucky.

"Never mind," whispered Puss. "I may be able to make your fortune, but first you must buy me some boots." So Jack took him to the boot shop.

Puss tried on all sorts of boots and shoes, and in the end he chose a pair of high boots, made from yellow leather. They made him look much taller.

"Now," he said to Jack, "you must buy me a bag that I can carry on my back."

So Jack took the cat to the scout supply shop and bought one of their finest knapsacks. It had leather straps and was waterproof.

That night Puss went to a lettuce field and filled his
bag with lettuces. He went into the woods and laid the
lettuces on the ground. Then he hid.

In no time at all, a fat rabbit appeared out of his hole and saw the line of lettuces. Being greedy as well as fat, the rabbit gobbled them up, not knowing how close he was getting to the cat.

Just as the rabbit was stretching out a paw for the last lettuce, Puss leaped out and caught him in the bag.

Chuckling to himself, Puss set off along a winding path, carefully following the signposts.

Soon the cat arrived at the king's castle and walked boldly up to the guard at the gate.

"No catsdogspigssheepormonsters allowed!" snapped the guard.

"May not a cat look at a king?" whispered Puss, and seeing no harm in it, the guard marched him toward the throne room. The king blinked to see a cat in yellow boots.

"Your Majesty," said Puss, bowing low, "please accept this fine rabbit, a gift from the estate of my master, the Marquis of Carabas."

The king was most impressed, both with the rabbit and the polite cat. "Do thank your master," he said, and the cat left the castle, a friend of the king's.

Puss trotted away, pleased with his work.

The next day Puss took some grain and made a trail of
it. Then he lay down and pretended to be dead. When
two partridges came along, eating the grain, he popped
them in his bag too.

Again he visited the king, saying that the partridges were gifts from his master. The king was well pleased. On his way out, Puss met the secretary and found out where the king's coach was to pass next day.

The next morning Puss told Jack that he was to swim in the river.

"Don't want to," sniffed Jack. "It'll be *freezing*!"

"Trust me, and remember that I'll make your fortune," wheedled the crafty cat. Jack, being a simple lad, agreed, and dived into the river.

It was freezing. "Funny way to make a fortune!" he gasped to Puss, who sat warm and dry on the bank.

Puss knew that the king's coach was going to pass that way, so when Jack wasn't looking, he hid his clothes, then ran into the road and stopped the royal coach.

"HELP! HELP!" he howled. "My master, the Marquis of Carabas, is drowning!"

The king jumped out of his coach, followed by his daughter. Waving his arms, he told the coachman to go and help the marquis.

"But he has no clothes!" said the cat. "His silks were stolen by a band of wicked thieves."

Of course, Jack's clothes were not really silk; they were the old rags he had worn for years.

When the coachmen returned with Jack, the lad was so cold, he couldn't speak. A chest of royal clothes was produced, and Jack was given a suit of the finest material. He looked every inch a marquis. When the king thanked him for the rabbit and the partridges, Jack hadn't the faintest idea what he was talking about, but he was too cold to argue. (Puss had found a very nice hat for himself.)

The king allowed Jack to ride in the royal coach, which pleased the princess, who was falling in love with the Marquis of Carabas.

As the coach went on its way the cat ran ahead, and soon he came to a wheatfield where harvesters were cutting the wheat.

"Listen!" shouted Puss, in his sternest voice. "When the royal coach comes by, you must say that all these fields belong to the Marquis of Carabas. If you don't, I'll come back and scratch you to bits. Okay?"

"Okay!" said the harvesters, badly frightened.

Puss then went on until he came across a goatherd.

"When the king comes by, you must tell him that these goats belong to the Marquis of Carabas. If you don't, I'll come back and pull your beard. Okay?"

"Okay!" gasped the surprised goatherd.

Puss rushed on his way, toward a white palace in the forest.

Puss strode right up to the front door of the palace and banged loudly on the knocker. It was a very brave thing to do, because a terrible ogre lived there. The ogre opened the door himself. (He had to, since he had eaten all his servants.)

The ogre didn't have many visitors on account of his bad temper, and he blinked to see a cat in yellow boots peeping in through his door.

"Greetings, Your Ugliness," smiled Puss. "I have long wanted to meet you. I have heard you can turn yourself into any animal you please. The thing is, I just don't believe it!"

The ogre couldn't believe his ears. He spluttered and coughed, and jumped up and down in a rage.

"*Gggglumph,* I can, I can too! *Glummmph,* I'll show—I'll show you, then I'll chew you!"

His hair grew, and slowly the ogre changed into a terrible lion.

With a leap the lion chased Puss up the chimney.

"Pooh! I don't think *that's* so smart," yelled Puss from the safety of the chimney. "Everyone can grow *big*! That's *easy*! Can't you do better? Can't you turn into something small?"

The lion seemed quite put out, so Puss dropped down out of the chimney.

"Like a mouse," the sneaky cat said with a grin. "Could you change into a mouse?"

"Er—yes, I think so," muttered the ogre. "But changing into lions is quite difficult, you know!"

The ogre grew smaller and smaller, and mousier and mousier.

When his roars turned into squeaks and he was really quite tiny, Puss pounced...

...and swallowed the terrible ogre in one mousy gulp!

In the meantime the king arrived at the wheatfields.

"To whom do these fields belong?" said the king to the harvesters.

"To the Marquis of Carabas," they answered.

Then the royal coach passed the goatherd, and the king asked who owned the fine goats.

"The Marquis of Carabas, sire," said the goatherd, shaking.

"You really are a most important marquis!" said the king to Jack, who still hadn't the faintest idea what he was talking about.

When the king arrived at the white palace, he was lost in admiration.

"Who owns this wonderful palace?" he said to Puss, who met them at the gate.

"The Marquis of Carabas, my master," said the cat.

Puss had prepared a banquet for the king, who, having eaten, turned to Jack and said:

"My dear Marquis of Carabas, all of this splendor is too much for a marquis. I will make you a prince."

Although Jack still didn't quite understand what was going on, he dropped to one knee, and the king tapped him on each shoulder.

"Arise, Jack, Prince of Carabas."

Of course, Jack married the king's daughter, and they lived long lives in the white palace. He loved the princess and enjoyed being a real prince. In gratitude, he made Puss the Master of the Prince's Household, and Grand Mouser in Chief...

...although he *still* didn't understand some of the things Puss did.

About the Author

Tony Ross is a popular illustrator who has been widely acclaimed for his versions of familiar folktales. His most recent book for Delacorte Press was *Jack and the Beanstalk*. Tony Ross lives in Cheshire, England, and teaches art at the Manchester Polytechnic School.

About the Book

The text of *Puss in Boots* is set in Tiffany Medium. The art was prepared in ink and watercolor. The book was printed by Grafiche AZ, Verona, Italy, and bound by the Economy Bookbinding Corporation in Kearny, New Jersey.